Follow That Ball

written by Margaret Crocker
illustrated by Andy Norman and Patrick Crouse

As soon as I reach
The best part of the beach,
I'll land in the sand,
And it will be grand.

Now it's time for fun,
For soaking up sun.
I'm ready to play,
And I have the whole day.

You can't catch me
When I'm by the sea.
I'm always in motion
When I'm at the ocean!

Then I slip.
Then I trip.
Then I fall.
Oh, my ball!

Now my bottom is wet,
And I'm kind of upset.
Plus I feel a sharp jab,
That might be a crab.

Worst of all,
WHERE'S MY BALL?

Here I am
With some bread and jam.

I've got a knack
For making a stack.

SMACK!

"This castle's a flop
    If we don't fix the top."

12

PLOP!

I've looked and it's clear
That my ball isn't here.
The shore is a bore
With no ball anymore.

I'll just have to ask.
Yes, that is my task.
I must ask one and all,
"Have you seen my ball?"

"Excuse me, Lou!
Has my ball rolled by you?
I'm asking around
So it can be found."

"Your ball slammed my head
And got sand on my bread.
Then it bounced off that way
Before I could say, 'HEY!'"

"Zweeble, my friend,
I'm at my wit's end!
Can you recall
If you've seen my ball?"

"Your ball whacked my stack
And didn't look back.
Then it bounced through the air
To land over there."

"Ella, at last!
  Has my ball been past?"
"Your ball's here, Denzel.
  It landed quite well!"

"Oh, you're right.
Wow, what a sight!
Come over here, guys.
You won't believe your eyes."

"Denzel saved the day
In the very best way.
His ball's just the thing
To give our castle some zing!"

"Whoa! What do you know?
I throw like a pro!
Hey, don't get me wrong.
That was my plan all along.